Hi-De-Hi

Written by **Marcia Vaughan**   Illustrated by **Kim Howard**

 GoodYearBooks

Uncle Marcos has a farm,

with a house and a field,

and a big, red barn.

Hi-de-hi, hi-de-ho.

Out in the pen you'll see a hog,

an orange cat,

and a yellow dog.

Hi-de-hi, hi-de-ho.

9

Out in the yard
you'll see a duck and three
red hens, "Cluck, cluck, cluck."

Hi-de-hi, hi-de-ho.

11

Out in the field you'll see a
sheep and spotted chicks,
"Peep, peep, peep."

Hi-de-hi, hi-de-ho.

Out in the barn you'll see
a cow and an old gray donkey
who pulls the plow.

Hi-de-hi,
hi-de-ho,
hi-de-hay!